Turkey Trot Plot

Don't miss a single

Nancy Drew Clue Book:

Pool Party Puzzler

Last Lemonade Standing

A Star Witness

Big Top Flop

Movie Madness

Pets on Parade

Candy Kingdom Chaos

World Record Mystery

Springtime Crime

Boo Crew

The Tortoise and the Scare

And coming soon:

Puppy Love Prank

Nancy Drew

CLUE BOOK

#12

Turkey Trot Plot

BY CAROLYN KEENE * ILLUSTRATED BY PETER FRANCIS

Aladdin

NEW YORK   LONDON   TORONTO   SYDNEY   NEW DELHI

ALADDIN

An imprint of Simon & Schuster Children's Publishing Division
1230 Avenue of the Americas, New York, New York 10020
First Aladdin paperback edition September 2019
Text copyright © 2019 by Simon & Schuster, Inc.
Illustrations copyright © 2019 by Peter Francis
Also available in an Aladdin hardcover edition.
ALADDIN and related logo are registered trademarks of Simon & Schuster, Inc.
NANCY DREW, NANCY DREW CLUE BOOK,
and colophons are registered trademarks off Simon & Schuster, Inc.
All rights reserved, including the right of reproduction in whole or in part in any form.
For information about special discounts for bulk purchases, please contact Simon & Schuster
Special Sales at 1-866-506-1949 or business@simonandschuster.com.
The Simon & Schuster Speakers Bureau can bring authors to your live event.
For more information or to book an event contact the Simon & Schuster Speakers Bureau
at 1-866-248-3049 or visit our website at www.simonspeakers.com.
Series designed by Karina Granda
Interior designed by Tom Daly
The illustrations for this book were rendered digitally.
The text of this book was set in Adobe Garamond Pro.
Manufactured in the United States of America 0819 OFF
2 4 6 8 10 9 7 5 3 1
Library of Congress Cataloging-in-Publication Data
Names: Keene, Carolyn, author. | Francis, Peter, 1973- illustrator.
Title: Turkey trot plot / by Carolyn Keene ; illustrated by Peter Francis.
Description: First Aladdin hardcover/paperback edition. | New York : Aladdin, 2019. | Series: Nancy
Drew clue book ; #12 | Summary: When a chocolate turkey—the intended prize for the winners of
a Thanksgiving Day race—disappears, Nancy and her friends identify and eliminate suspects in their
search for the missing confection.
Identifiers: LCCN 2018037419 (print) | LCCN 2018043917 (eBook) |
ISBN 9781534431317 (eBook) | ISBN 9781534431300 (hc) | ISBN 9781534431294 (pbk)
Subjects: | CYAC: Chocolate—Fiction. | Lost and found possessions—Fiction. |
Mystery and detective stories.
Classification: LCC PZ7.K23 (eBook) | LCC PZ7.K23 Tu 2019 (print) | DDC [Fic]—dc23
LC record available at https://lccn.loc.gov/2018037419

* CONTENTS *

Chapter

1

GOBBLER WOBBLER

"Nope," Bess Marvin said, shaking her head. "Those feathers are wrong. Totally wrong."

"But they're such pretty colors, Bess," eight-year-old Nancy Drew said, holding the plastic bag of feathers in her hand.

"Feathers are feathers," George Fayne insisted.

It was Wednesday afternoon. Nancy and her best friends had gone straight from school to Chippy's Craft Market to buy feathers. But not just any feathers . . .

"Those are hen feathers," Bess said, pointing to the label on the bag. "We're running in a Turkey Trot tomorrow, not a Hen Heat."

George sighed as she grabbed another bag from the shelf. The feathers in this one were long and white with a brown stripy design. "Totally turkey," she said. "Happy yet?"

Bess read the label on the bag out loud: "One dozen synthetic turkey feathers. What does 'syn-thet-ic' mean?"

"I think it means 'fake,'" Nancy said.

"Good enough," George said, tossing the bag into their shopping basket. "Now that we found the right feathers, what do we do with them?"

Reaching into her backpack, Bess pulled out a fashion sketch. "Here's my design for our Turkey Trot costumes," she explained. "All we have to do is glue turkey feathers around the necks of sweat-shirts and on leggings. Then we glue a few feath-ers on our headbands."

Bess ran her hand over the sketch and said, "Simple . . . yet elegant!"

"Simple?" George scoffed. "What's so simple about gluing hundreds of feathers one by one?"

Nancy liked Bess's design but agreed with George. Gluing so many feathers would take forever. "There's got to be a quicker way," she said.

George's dark curls bounced as she tilted her head in thought. "Here's an idea," she said with a grin. "We squirt sticky maple syrup all over our clothes, dump feathers in front of a fan, turn it on, and—whoosh!"

"I say let's dump that idea, George," Bess said.

Nancy giggled. Bess and George were cousins but as different as turkey and peacock feathers. Bess was a serious fashionista who loved the newest styles. George was a tech geek and proud of it. Her style was jeans and sneakers—definitely not turkey costumes.

"Why do we have to trot in goofy costumes anyway?" George asked as they filled their basket with more turkey feather bags.

"That's the whole idea of the Turkey Trot tomorrow," Nancy explained. "The kid or team with the best turkey costume wins a giant chocolate turkey."

"Not just any chocolate turkey, Nancy," Bess reminded her. "This one is from Classy Coco, the fancy new chocolate store on Main Street."

"I've never tasted Classy Coco's chocolate," Nancy said, "but everyone says it's amazing."

"Just remember our deal, you guys," George said. "If our team wins, we split the chocolate turkey into three pieces—"

"For our Thanksgiving dinners tomorrow," Nancy cut in excitedly. "Go, Galloping Gobblers!"

This wasn't the first time Nancy, Bess, and George had teamed up. They also had their own detective club called the Clue Crew. Nancy even had a clue book to write down all their clues and suspects.

"Let's buy the feathers before it gets late," Nancy said. She was about to pick up their basket when—

"Yodel-ay-ee-oooooo . . . Yodel-ay-ee-ooooo!"

The girls froze at the strange sound.

"What was that?" Bess asked.

"It doesn't sound like a turkey gobbling," George said.

"Yodel-ay-ee-ooooo!" There it was again!

Nancy, Bess, and George followed the yodeling to the next aisle. There they saw a girl looking at packaged ribbons.

She was dressed in an embroidered skirt and a puffy-sleeved blouse. Over her blouse was a black velvet vest, and on her blond braided hair was a green felt hat.

To Nancy she looked like a girl from a Swiss storybook. She also looked familiar . . .

"You guys," Nancy said while the girl kept yodeling. "Isn't that Shelby Metcalf?"

"But Shelby doesn't have long blond hair like me," Bess said. "That girl does."

"Or braids either," George said.

Shelby turned to the girls and smiled. "It's a wig," she said. "I just need to tie on a few ribbons and I'm all set!"

"Cool," George said. "But what's with the Heidi costume?"

"Shouldn't you be shopping for a turkey costume?" Nancy asked. "The Turkey Trot is tomorrow, on Thanksgiving morning."

"I'm not running in the Trot," Shelby said. "I have to get ready for the Pixie Scout International Food Fest on Friday."

"International Food Fest?" Nancy repeated. "You mean there will be food from other countries?"

"Everyone in my troop is bringing a different dish to taste," Shelby explained. "I've been wearing my costume the past few days to get into character." Shelby opened her mouth to yodel again.

To stop her, George quickly cut in. "What food are you bringing, Shelby?" she asked.

"I'm making a Swiss chocolate fondue," Shelby said proudly. "It's where you dip marshmallows, fruit, and pretzels into a pot of melted chocolate. I'm using melted Choco-Wacko bars!"

"Yummy," Bess said. "But too bad the chocolate isn't from Classy Coco."

"You mean that fancy chocolate store on Main Street?" Shelby asked. "What's so special about that place?"

"My mom is a caterer and told me all about it," George said. "Classy Coco is owned by a woman named Anna Epicure. She used to be the editor of a magazine called *Bon-Bon Vivant*. It's all about chocolate."

"The chocolates in Anna's store are like little statues!" Nancy explained. "I heard she has them made at fancy chocolate factories all over the world!"

"Wow!" Shelby exclaimed. "Forget the Choco-Wacko bars. I'll use Classy Coco chocolate in my fondue!"

"Good luck." George sighed. "One chocolate bar at Classy Coco is the price of fifty Choco-Wacko bars."

"You'd have to sell a lot of lemonade to buy that, Shelby," Bess said. "And it's getting too cold for lemonade."

Shelby's shoulders drooped as she muttered, "Phooey."

"I'm sure your fondue will be great anyway," Nancy said.

"Great isn't enough, Nancy," Shelby said. "My chocolate fondue has to be perfect—no matter what I have to do!"

Shelby tossed a braid over her shoulder and walked away.

"She forgot the ribbons," Bess said. "Ribbons would go great with her costume."

"So would a goat," George joked.

The girls headed straight to the check-out counter. Bess used her Chippy's birthday gift card to buy the turkey feathers.

"Mission accomplished," Bess declared as the girls left the store. "Now let's go home and work on our costumes."

Nancy, Bess, and George walked up Main

Street on their way home. Each girl had the same rule: They could walk anywhere as long as it was less than five blocks and as long as they walked together. That was more fun anyway!

"What's that smell?" George asked.

"I didn't use the strawberry shampoo you hate," Bess said, "if that's what you mean."

Nancy noticed the sweet smell too. But it wasn't strawberries. "It's chocolate!" she said excitedly. "I'll bet it's coming from Classy Coco down the block!"

Nancy, Bess, and George neared the store. They could see a reporter and a camerawoman from Station WRIV-TV standing outside. Also in front of the store was a woman with short dark hair.

"It's Anna Epicure," George whispered. "I saw her picture online."

The girls could hear the reporter ask, "What makes you think you can run a successful chocolate store, Anna?"

"I once ran a successful chocolate magazine,

didn't I?" Anna replied. "Running a chocolate store will be a piece of cake."

Anna turned to the camera and quickly added, "Speaking of cake . . . try my black forest cake truffles—they're fabulous!"

Nancy, Bess, and George wanted to see the chocolates with their own eyes. So while the reporter asked more questions, they slipped inside Classy Coco.

The first things the girls noticed were framed *Bon-Bon Vivant* magazine covers on the walls. The best things were the chocolate figurines wrapped in clear plastic and tied with ribbons.

"There's a chocolate Empire State Building!" Nancy said.

"My eyes spy a chocolate computer!" George said. She then pointed to a brown wedge carved with holes. "That looks like a chocolate hunk of cheese!"

"I'm glad it's not real cheese," Bess said, squeezing her nose shut. "I hate stinky cheese more than anything!"

They were about to check out a chocolate kitten when—

"Omigosh!" a girl's voice gasped. "It's more awesome than I imagined!"

A small crowd of kids rushed into the store to surround a chocolate turkey on a pedestal.

"There's the chocolate turkey prize," George said. "But who are those kids?"

"The tallest girl is Hazel Hookstratten,"

Nancy whispered. "She's president of the Choco Chewers Club."

"You mean the Chocolate Lovers Club?" Bess whispered. "Where they meet every other Saturday to eat chocolate?"

"To eat—and worship chocolate!" George said.

Nancy saw what George meant. Hazel was hugging the pedestal while shouting, "Be still, my trembling taste buds! Be still!"

Hazel's taste buds weren't the only things trembling. As she hugged the pedestal, the chocolate turkey began to tip!

A boy from the club, Lester Chin, waved his arms in the air. "Look out, Hazel!" he shouted. "That gobbler is a wobbler!"

Chapter

PRIZE SURPRISE

Everyone froze as the magnificent chocolate turkey wobbled back and forth on the pedestal—everyone but George, who leaped forward for the catch!

"Gotcha!" George exclaimed, grabbing the turkey before it could fall.

Nancy breathed a sigh of relief, causing her reddish-blond bangs to flutter. "Good catch, George," she said.

"Hey," George said with a grin, "it's soccer season."

Carefully, Nancy and Bess took the chocolate turkey from George. They placed it back on the pedestal, made sure it was steady, then stepped back.

"Thanks for saving the chocolate turkey, George," Hazel said. "What was I thinking, hugging it like that?"

Nancy knew what Hazel was thinking. Like the other club members, Hazel loved chocolate more than anything. When everyone else in the school cafeteria ate tuna and peanut butter sandwiches, Hazel ate *pain au chocolat*—a fancy French chocolate sandwich.

"Are you all running in the Turkey Trot tomorrow?" Nancy asked. "I'll bet you really want to win this chocolate turkey."

"We're running," Hazel said. "But our costumes will never win."

Hazel shot Lester a hard glance. "We had

awesome costumes decorated with chocolate feathers," she said. "Tell them what happened, Lester."

"I left the costumes in front of a sunny window in the clubhouse," Lester confessed. "When we got back, the chocolate feathers had melted."

A member named Gillian shook her head. "We ordered those feathers from a chocolate store in New York," she said, "and it's too late to get more."

"It wasn't totally my fault," Lester insisted. "The weatherman said it would be cloudy with a chance of rain!"

"Don't worry," Nancy told the club with a smile. "I'm sure your new costumes will be—"

"Step away from the chocolate turkey!" a woman's voice demanded. "Step away now!"

The kids spun around. Anna Epicure was walking into her store, a worried look on her face.

"We were just admiring your chocolate turkey, Ms. Epicure," Hazel said. "We're the Choco Chewers Club of River Heights."

"Our club reads your magazine," Lester told Anna. "All it needs are crossword puzzles and riddles and it would be my favorite!"

"Riddles?" Anna said, narrowing her eyes. "Here's one: What's under twelve years old and has to be extra careful around my fine chocolates?"

"Um," Lester said, "is the answer . . . kids?"

"Riiiiight," Anna said.

Nancy and the others stepped back from the chocolate turkey. She hoped Anna hadn't seen it topple off the pedestal.

"Ms. Epicure," Nancy asked, "is this turkey made from dark chocolate or milk chocolate?"

"There is only one kind of chocolate in my store," Anna replied. "Classy."

"In that case," George said, "can we have some classy free samples?"

"Samples?" Anna gasped. "Sorry, but I don't believe in samples. Everyone in River Heights knows my chocolate is the best."

"Excuse me," a boy's voice asked, "but did someone say . . . samples?!"

Everyone turned to see a boy carrying a tray filled with paper cups into the store. Nancy, Bess, and George recognized the boy as Henderson Murphy from their third-grade class.

"Try my dad's latest hot chocolate flavor," Henderson said with a grin. "It's called Minty Martian!"

George looked into one of the cups. "The hot chocolate is green," she said. "So are the marshmallows."

"Green like a Martian," Henderson said with a grin. "That was my idea!"

"I've never seen a Martian," Hazel said. "And I thought your dad sold ice cream."

"Ice cream when it's hot," Henderson said, "hot chocolate and cookies when it's cold."

Anna planted both hands on her hips. "I told your father not to park his truck in front of my store," she told Henderson. "Everyone will think his hot chocolate comes from Classy Coco!"

"What's wrong with that?" Henderson asked.

"I don't sell hot chocolate," Anna declared.

"Fine chocolate should be nipped, not sipped!"

The Mr. Drippy truck outside began playing its musical jingle. Nancy, Bess, and George heard it loud and clear inside the store. So did Anna . . .

"I think you children should leave," Anna told them. "I have to wrap the chocolate turkey in plastic."

"Why is all your chocolate in plastic bags?" Bess asked.

"Airtight plastic keeps it fresh," Anna explained. "That and cool temperatures, especially overnight."

The kids took one last look at the chocolate turkey, all wanting to win it the next day. They then filed out of the store to taste Henderson's Minty Martian samples.

"It's great for green hot chocolate," Nancy said after a sip.

"You bet it is," Henderson said. "I'll show that snooty Anna Epicure. Just you wait!"

Nancy wondered what Henderson meant. As he continued to give out samples, George whispered, "You guys, check out what I have in my pocket."

"What?" Nancy asked.

George looked both ways before holding up a small chunk of chocolate. "It's a piece of the Classy Coco turkey!"

"Omigosh, George!" Bess gasped. "You didn't break it off the turkey, did you?"

"Nah," George said. "It broke off in my hand as I caught the turkey. It's from the bottom part, so hopefully Anna won't notice."

George broke the chunk into three smaller pieces. Nancy, Bess, and George tasted the chocolate turkey, their eyes wide.

"Best. Chocolate. Ever!" Bess declared.

"Better than a Choco-Wacko bar!" George said.

"It's for sure a winner," Nancy agreed with a smile. "That's why tomorrow—the Galloping Gobblers have got to win."

"Yeah," George said. "So we can gobble up that turkey!"

Thanksgiving morning couldn't come fast enough for Nancy, Bess, and George. At ten o'clock they were on Main Street in their turkey costumes, ready to trot. The busiest street in River Heights had been closed just for the event.

George tugged at the feathers around the neck of her sweatshirt. "I don't know if we look like turkeys," she groaned, "but I sure feel like one."

As the girls walked to the starting point,

Nancy saw Shelby. Their friend was walking the other way on the sidewalk dressed in her Swiss costume and carrying a shopping bag.

"Hi, Shelby!" Nancy called. "Buying more Choco-Wacko bars for your fondue tomorrow?"

"Can't talk now!" Shelby called back, her voice cracking. "I've got to go!"

As Shelby quickened her pace, Bess said, "That was weird. Shelby always talks to us."

"She's probably nervous about the International Food Fest tomorrow," Nancy said. "She wants her fondue to be perfect."

The girls joined the other trotters and saw Hazel and her club. They wore collars made from blue and green feathers.

"Pretty feathers," Nancy told Hazel. "Did you buy them at Chippy's Craft Mart?"

Hazel shook her head. "We plucked them off feather dusters from Harry's Hardware Store," she said.

Nancy, Bess, and George stood with the others at the starting point. Their knees jumped with excitement as they waited for the announcement. Finally it came . . .

"On your mark . . . get set . . . trot!"

Nancy, Bess, and George trotted forward along with the others. Many of the trotters gobbled as they ran the three blocks to the finish line in front of the Classy Coco chocolate store. Mayor Stone stood there holding a microphone. . . .

"Congratulations on crushing the Turkey Trot, kids," the mayor told the crowd. "I hope you like chocolate, because it's time for the chocolate turkey prize!"

Everyone turned to see the Classy Coco door fly open. Ann Epicure hurried out, but she didn't have the chocolate turkey—just an armful of magazines!

"Mayor Strong," Anna said, her eyebrows furrowed. "I'm afraid there will be no chocolate turkey for the winners."

Confused whispers filled the air. Nancy, Bess, and George looked at each other with surprise. Did they just hear what they thought they heard?

"No chocolate turkey?" Mayor Strong asked. "Why not?"

"Because, Mayor Strong," Anna declared, "it's gone!"

Chapter

PRANKS-GIVING

Confused whispers became gasps. Nancy turned to Bess and George. "How could the chocolate turkey be gone?" she cried. "We just saw it yesterday!"

Mayor Strong raised both hands to quiet the crowd. Anna leaned in to the microphone to explain. . . .

"I got to my store this morning at nine o'clock," Anna explained. "The chocolate turkey was on its pedestal, wrapped and ready for the Turkey Trot."

"Yes? And?" Mayor Strong urged.

"A bit later I went to the back room to check an order," Anna went on. "When I came back, the chocolate turkey was nowhere in the store!"

Mayor Strong forced a smile and said, "No worries, Ms. Epicure. Surely you can present the winner with another chocolate masterpiece."

"I'm afraid that's impossible, Mayor," Anna said, holding out the magazines. "Instead please take two past issues of *Bon-Bon Vivant* magazine, autographed by me."

The kids groaned with disappointment. Anna turned to them with a frown. "Oh, boo-hoo," she said. "If it weren't for you kids, my turkey wouldn't be missing."

"I'm afraid I don't understand, Anna," Mayor Strong said. "What do the kids have to do with the missing turkey?"

"I allowed too many children into my store yesterday to admire the chocolate turkey," Anna explained. "I'm almost sure it gave them ideas."

"Did you hear that?" George asked Nancy

and Bess. "Anna thinks a kid stole the turkey!"

Anna turned toward her store. Before walking in, she flipped over a sign dangling from the doorknob. It read, NO CHILDREN ALLOWED.

"No kids allowed?" a girl in the crowd shouted after Anna slammed the door shut.

"That's not fair!" a boy exclaimed.

Nancy agreed. It wasn't fair. When everyone calmed down, Mayor Strong announced the winner of the costume contest. It was four girls dressed as turkey ballerinas.

The feathered ballerinas accepted their issues of *Bon-Bon Vivant* magazine with strained smiles. Nancy, Bess, and George quietly slipped out of the crowd.

"How can such a big chocolate turkey just disappear?" Bess asked.

"I know how," George said. "Someone came into the store while Anna was in the back and took it."

"But who?" Nancy wondered.

"'Who' rhymes with 'clue,'" Bess said. She

tapped her chin thoughtfully and smiled. "Hmm. Could this be another case for the Clue Crew?"

Nancy pulled her clue book from a small cross-body bag. "Does this answer your question?" she asked. "Even if a kid did take the turkey, it's not fair for Anna to blame all the kids."

"If we find the person who took the chocolate turkey," George said, "maybe we can talk Anna into letting kids back into the store."

"What's a candy store without kids?" Bess asked.

Nancy, Bess, and George walked to a bench and sat down. Nancy opened her clue book to a clean page. She pulled out a pen with purple ink to draw a picture of the chocolate turkey. Next to that she drew a question mark.

"Let's start with a timeline," Nancy said. "When do you think the chocolate turkey went missing?"

"Anna said it was there this morning when she got to the store at nine o'clock," George told them. "Then she left for a bit, and it was gone when she came back."

"We got to the finish line at about ten thirty," Nancy pointed out. "So the chocolate turkey had to disappear between nine and that time."

Nancy wrote the time line in her clue book. She then looked up and said, "Should we start a suspect list or look for clues?"

"Let's look for clues inside Classy Coco," George said.

"How?" Bess asked. "Anna won't allow kids in the store."

"She can't keep us from looking in," George

said with a grin. After leading the way to Classy Coco, George kneeled outside the door. She leaned forward to peek through the mail slot.

"Rats!" George grumbled.

"Rats?!" Bess gasped. "You see rats in the store?!"

"No, Bess," George said. "All I can see is the floor."

"But do you see anything on the floor?" Nancy asked.

"Actually I do!" George said, still looking. "I see feathers. One blue and two green."

"I didn't see feathers on the floor yesterday," Nancy said.

"Are they turkey feathers, George?" Bess asked. "Or hen feathers, chicken feathers, pigeon feathers—"

"Who knows, Bess?" George answered. "They're just feathers."

"But it's an awesome clue, George," Nancy said. "The Choco Chewers were wearing collars with blue and green feathers."

"The club didn't think their costumes would win," George pointed out. "Maybe they came up with another way to get the chocolate turkey."

"A bad way," Bess added.

A few kids stopped to stare at George by the mail slot, so the girls decided to leave. Nancy started the suspect list with the Choco Chewers Club. But Bess wasn't so sure . . .

"I didn't see a Choco Chewer holding a big bag at the Turkey Trot," Bess said. "Where else would they stash a stolen chocolate turkey?"

"Maybe one of the club members took off with the turkey," George said. "It's not like we did a Choco Chewers head count."

The mention of a big bag had made Nancy's eyes light up. "We saw Shelby on Main Street carrying a big bag," she blurted.

"Shelby wanted her chocolate fondue to be perfect," George reminded them.

"Her hat had feathers in it too," Bess said. "But I can't remember what colors."

Nancy tapped her chin with the top of her

pen. It always helped her think. "So if a fondue is a pot of melted chocolate," she said, "maybe Shelby's fondue is a melted chocolate turkey!"

"From Classy Coco!" George added. "Write Shelby's name, Nancy."

"Don't, Nancy," Bess said. "Shelby is our friend!"

"I know, Bess," Nancy said. "But as my dad says, even friends can make mistakes."

Nancy added Shelby's name to the suspect list. She then shut her clue book and said, "I have to go home and help with Thanksgiving dinner. I'm in charge of decorating the pumpkin pie."

"Let's meet Friday to work on this case," George said.

"I'll bring my clue book," Nancy promised.

"And some leftover pumpkin pie, please!" Bess giggled.

When Nancy got home, Hannah Gruen already had the pie ingredients on the counter. Hannah was the Drews' housekeeper, but she was much more like a mother to Nancy. She made sure Nancy did her homework, brushed her teeth, and ate healthy foods. And since pumpkins were a vegetable—pumpkin pie made the cut!

"Fill the pie crust to the top, Nancy," Hannah directed, "and try not to let it drip over the sides."

Nancy's chocolate Labrador puppy, Chocolate Chip, watched hungrily as Nancy spooned pumpkin filling into the crust. But her mind was filled with thoughts of the Clue Crew's new case. Who took the chocolate turkey from Classy Coco?

"I have two suspects so far," Nancy said. "Two is good, but the Clue Crew likes to have three."

Mr. Drew was at the oven checking on the turkey. "I have a favor to ask, Nancy," he said, peeking through the glass oven door.

"Do you need me to grate cheese for the broccoli casserole, Daddy?" Nancy asked.

Mr. Drew smiled and said, "I need you to please not discuss your new case anymore tonight. Our guests, Mr. and Mrs. Diaz, might want to talk about something else."

"Like football." Hannah chuckled. "The Diazes love football."

"Oh," Nancy said.

"So what do you think, Nancy?" Mr. Drew asked. "Even detectives need a break once in a while. Deal?"

Nancy gave it some thought. Her dad was a lawyer and often helped her with the Clue Crew's cases. But she had already told him and Hannah everything there was to know about the missing chocolate turkey. So—

"Deal!" Nancy declared.

"Are you sure you can do it, Detective Drew?" Hannah teased.

"Watch me, Hannah!" Nancy said with a smile.

"And by the way," Hannah said, "Mr. Diaz has a nut allergy, so I didn't buy walnuts for the pumpkin pie garnish."

"What do we use instead, Hannah?" Nancy asked.

"Marshmallows," Hannah said, holding up a bag of mini marshmallows, "shaped like little fall leaves!"

Chip barked her approval. Nancy liked them too. "Perfect!" she declared.

Nancy was about to add another spoon of pumpkin when she remembered the Minty Martian hot chocolate with green marshmallows. And something else . . .

Omigosh, Nancy thought. *Henderson Murphy!*

Chapter

CHOCO-NO-NO

Nancy kept spooning as her head spun with thoughts of Henderson. . . .

Anna had said not-so-nice things about Henderson's dad's hot chocolate, Nancy thought, *and he said he'd show her!*

What did Henderson mean by that? Did he mean he'd take Anna's prize chocolate turkey to get even?

"Nancy, the pie crust!" Hannah called.

"Huh?" Nancy glanced down to see pumpkin

oozing over the pastry crust. She had been so focused on Henderson, she'd forgotten about the pie!

"Something on your mind, Nancy?" Mr. Drew asked.

Nancy looked up from the messy counter. Telling her dad about Henderson would mean breaking their deal.

"Um, no, Daddy," Nancy said. "Could you please pass the suspect—I mean—paper towels?"

Oops! Nancy knew she'd promised not to talk about her case. But she didn't promise not to think about it!

"I should have taped the Thanksgiving Parade on TV yesterday morning," Bess said. "I heard that the Ginger Girls sang 'Ship of Love'—on a real live pirate ship float!"

Nancy smiled. The Ginger Girls was one of their favorite singing groups.

"We were too busy Turkey Trotting yesterday morning to enjoy the parade." George groaned.

"My neck still itches from all those feathers!"

"But thanks to the Turkey Trot," Nancy said, "we have a brand-new mystery to solve!"

It was Friday morning. The Clue Crew was walking to the park to discuss their case. Nancy had already shared some leftover pumpkin pie with her friends. She had also shared her thoughts on Henderson Murphy.

"Would Henderson really take a chocolate turkey from a fancy store?" George asked.

"Well, there's only one way to find out," Bess told her.

The girls stopped at the sound of the Mr. Drippy truck. It was parked near the park's main gate.

"Henderson usually rides with his dad when there's no school," Nancy said. "Let's ask Mr. Murphy where he was yesterday morning during the Turkey Trot."

But when the girls looked for Henderson, his dad shook his head. "I'm afraid Henderson is home in bed, girls," he said. "He got sick yesterday."

Nancy was about to ask about Henderson

when a boy and girl rushed up to the truck window.

"One cup of Minty Martian, please!" the boy said.

"Make that two," the girl said excitedly.

"Two Minty Martians, coming right up!" Mr. Murphy said. As he got busy pouring hot chocolate, the Clue Crew walked away from the truck.

"I wonder why Henderson is sick," Bess said.

"He probably has a stomachache," George said. "Too much Thanksgiving turkey."

Turkey? Nancy stopped walking, her eyes lighting up.

"Too much Thanksgiving turkey?" Nancy asked slowly. "Or too much chocolate turkey?"

Chapter

5

YODEL-AY-EE-CLUE!

"What do you mean, Nancy?" Bess asked.

"What does the missing turkey have to do with Henderson being sick?" George wanted to know.

"If Henderson did take the chocolate turkey," Nancy said, "maybe he ate it to destroy the evidence."

"A whole chocolate turkey?" Bess said, wrinkling her nose. "That's too much even for me."

"It might be the reason why Henderson got sick," Nancy said.

"What about the feathers we saw in Classy Coco?" George asked. "If Henderson wasn't in the Turkey Trot, how could they be from him?"

"I don't know," Nancy admitted as she scribbled the new discovery in her clue book. "That's why we have to go to the Murphy house and talk to Henderson."

"Nuh-uh!" George exclaimed. "What if he hurls all over us? He might have a stomachache, remember?"

"We'll go later, when he's feeling better," Nancy suggested. "In the meantime let's investigate Shelby at the Pixie Scout International Food Fest. It's today, and we have to check out her chocolate fondue."

"How will we know if the melted chocolate in her fondue pot is the melted chocolate turkey?" Bess asked.

"We already tasted the chocolate turkey," Nancy pointed out. "Now we have to taste the melted chocolate in Shelby's pot to see if it's a match."

"Tasting chocolate?" George said with a grin. "I am so loving this case!"

"How do we know what time the Food Fest is," Bess asked, "and where it's being held?"

"I looked it up online last night," George said. "It's at one o'clock today in the school gym. There's just one problem."

"What?" Nancy asked.

"It's for Pixie Scouts and their families only," George said. "How will we get in?"

"Too bad we don't have Pixie Scout uniforms," Bess said. "They'd let us in then."

"Maybe we don't need uniforms," George said. "Maybe the Pixie Scouts will be wearing costumes from other countries like Shelby."

"So where do we get costumes from other countries?" Nancy wanted to know.

"From my mom," George said. "She has a bunch of international hats from a party she catered last year."

"I love hats!" Bess said excitedly.

"I love that idea," Nancy said with a smile. "Thanks, George. It might work!"

"Remind me what I'm supposed to be," George whispered, adjusting the round black hat on her head.

"You're a gaucho, George," Nancy whispered back. "It's like a cowboy in Argentina."

"And I'm a little Dutch girl," Bess said, gazing up at her crisp white cap. "I just wish I had a pair of wooden shoes, too."

"What am I, a fashion outlet?" George asked. "Be happy I could get us these hats."

The shiny gold Thai hat on Nancy's head wobbled back and forth as they walked to the school lunchroom. "Remember," she said, "we have to pretend we're Pixie Scouts, not detectives."

River Heights Elementary School was closed for Thanksgiving weekend, but the lunchroom was open for the Pixie Scout International Food Fest.

When the woman at the door saw Nancy, Bess, and George, she smiled. "Don't you girls look nice? Go right on in and enjoy the Food Fest."

"*Dank je!*" Bess said cheerily. "That's Dutch for 'thank you!'"

As they walked past the woman into the lunchroom, George whispered, "Are we lucky or what? We're in!"

"Where's Shelby?" Nancy asked, looking around.

The girls saw other Pixie Scouts standing behind tables in their costumes. While guests sampled the dishes, the Pixie Scouts talked about the countries they came from.

"Look—there's Shelby," Bess said. "And her mom."

Nancy looked to see where Bess was pointing. Mrs. Metcalf was helping Shelby set up a shiny red fondue pot. Behind the table was a colorful backdrop of the Swiss Alps.

"What if my fondue gets cold, Mom?" Shelby was asking as she flipped a braid from her wig. "Why couldn't I bring in a hot plate?"

"You're not allowed to have heated objects, Shelby," Mrs. Metcalf reminded her. "I'll run to the car for a towel. Maybe we can wrap the pot to keep it warm."

Mrs. Metcalf walked away. Shelby turned her attention to a big container, which she struggled to open. Nancy guessed it held fruit and marshmallows to dip in the melted chocolate.

"Hi, Shelby," Nancy said as the Clue Crew walked over.

"Nice setup," George added.

When Shelby saw Nancy, Bess, and George, her eyes widened with surprise. "What are you guys doing here?" she asked. "You're not Pixie Scouts."

"We are today," Bess said. "May we taste the melted chocolate in your fondue pot, please?"

"Chocolate?" Shelby gulped. She shook her head hard. "You can't. You can't, okay?"

"Why not?" George asked, raising an eyebrow. "Because the chocolate in the pot is from Classy Coco?"

"Classy Coco?" Shelby said as she placed the closed container on the table. "I don't know what you're talking about."

"Here's a hint," Bess said. "I'll bet everyone in this room can't wait to GOBBLE up your chocolate fondue."

Shelby stared at Bess. "Okay, this is getting weird."

"Or," Bess said, "maybe there's extra chocolate in that container you're trying to open."

Bess touched the lid of the container. Shelby grabbed it away fast. So fast the lid popped off, tipping the container and spilling most of its contents on the table and floor!

"Arrgh!" Shelby wailed. "See what you made me do?"

"Sorry, Shelby," Bess said. "I just wanted to see what was inside."

Nancy saw what was inside—and it wasn't what she thought. Instead of sweet snacks like strawberries, pineapple, and marshmallows, there were pieces of cauliflower, broccoli, carrots, and cubes of toast!

Shelby took off her Swiss hat and placed it on the table. She then slipped underneath to pick up some dropped carrots.

"You guys," Nancy whispered, "I don't think Shelby melted the chocolate turkey for the fondue."

"Why not?" George asked.

"Because," Nancy whispered, pointing to the covered pot, "I don't think it's chocolate!"

Chapter

6

CHEESE WHIZ!

"What do you mean, it's not chocolate?" George whispered. "Shelby told us she'd be making a chocolate fondue."

"We heard it with our own ears!" Bess whispered.

Nancy pointed to the veggies from the container. "People don't dip vegetables into chocolate fondue," she said. "And Shelby has a lot of veggies."

"I just noticed something else," Bess said,

nodding at Shelby's hat on the table. "The feathers in her hat are red and yellow, not blue and green."

"Then what's in the pot?" George asked.

"What are you whispering about?" Shelby asked as she pulled herself out from under the table.

"Sorry, Shelby," Nancy said. "We thought you were making a chocolate fondue."

"I wish it was chocolate!" Shelby groaned.

"It's not?" Bess asked.

Shelby shook her head. "My brother and his friends ate all of my Choco-Wacko bars on Wednesday night," she explained. "I didn't want to take a chance buying more chocolate, so I bought cheese. My brother hates cheese."

"I just hate the stinky kind," Bess said.

"I didn't tell you because I felt like a loser." Shelby sighed. "Even if it wasn't my fault."

Shelby gazed at her covered pot and said, "I wanted my chocolate fondue to be perfect. Instead . . . it's cheesy."

"Most people love melted cheese, Shelby," Nancy said. "It's the best part of a grilled cheese sandwich."

"What kind of cheese is it?" George asked. "The kind they put on cheeseburgers or pizza?"

"There was only one cheese in the supermarket on Thanksgiving morning," Shelby said, pulling the lid off the pot. "Limburger!"

Whoa! The strong smell made Nancy's and George's heads whip back. But it made Bess clap her hand over her nose and gag. "Ewwwwww! Stinky cheese! Stinky cheese!"

People in the room turned to stare at Bess.

"Bess, stop!" Shelby hissed. "Everyone will think my fondue is yucky, not just stinky!"

"I can't help it," Bess cried, squeezing her nose. "Eww, eww, eww!"

Nancy knew she

had to think fast. She turned to Shelby and said, "Quick! Start yodeling—loud!"

"Okay!" Shelby said. She threw back her shoulders and cried, "Yodel-ay-ee-oooo! Yodel-ay-ee-ooo!"

Shelby's yodels drowned out Bess's eww's. While guests smiled and applauded, Nancy and George hustled Bess out of the lunchroom and the school!

"Give me a break, Bess," George said when they were outside. "That cheese was strong, but it didn't smell bad."

"If you like stinky feet." Bess groaned.

"It's okay, you guys," Nancy said. "At least we found out that Shelby didn't take the chocolate turkey from Classy Coco!"

Nancy opened her clue book and crossed off Shelby's name. Now they had two suspects left on their list: Henderson Murphy and the Choco Chewers Club.

"Let's drop by Henderson's house first," Bess suggested. "His house is just two blocks from here."

"While I ask Henderson questions," Nancy said, shutting her clue book, "you can look around his room for clues."

"Can we drop these hats off first?" George asked. "Halloween was over a few weeks ago."

The Clue Crew brought their hats back to George's house. While they grabbed a snack in the kitchen, Nancy spotted a leftover fruit platter from the Faynes' Thanksgiving dinner.

"Can we bring this fruit platter to Henderson?" Nancy asked George. "To make it look like a get-well visit?"

"Instead of a snoop visit?" George joked. "I'll ask my mom."

The fruit platter was a go. George carried it the few blocks to the Murphy house, where Nancy rang the doorbell. Mrs. Murphy opened the door.

"Hello, Mrs. Murphy," Nancy said. "We heard Henderson is sick, so we want to give him this fruit."

George held out the platter and Mrs. Murphy smiled.

"Of course you can give it to him, girls," Mrs. Murphy said. "Come inside and go right up to his room."

As the girls climbed the stairs, Mrs. Henderson called, "Henderson's still sick, so don't get too close to him!"

"Yeah, in case he hurls," George whispered.

"Shhh!" Nancy whispered.

Once upstairs the girls found a door with the letter *H* nailed to it.

"Is that Henderson's room?" Bess asked.

"Unless he has a brother named Harvey," George said.

The door was half open, so Nancy, Bess, and George peeked inside. Henderson's bed was empty.

"Henderson's not in there," Bess said softly. "What do we do?"

"We go inside and look for clues," Nancy said.

Trying not to make noise, the Clue Crew entered Henderson's room. As George placed the fruit platter on Henderson's desk, she spotted something else. . . .

"You guys, check it out!" George said.

Nancy looked to see where George was pointing. Near the edge of Henderson's desk was a bright blue feather.

"Look what I found!" Bess said, pointing to the floor. "A green feather!"

"Those are the same colors as the feathers in Classy Coco," Nancy said excitedly. "But where did they come from?"

"Maybe we'll find out," George said. "Let's look for more clues before Henderson gets back."

The girls spread out to search the room. Next to Henderson's bed Nancy found a wastebasket filled with crumpled tissues. Also next to his bed was a machine spewing a soft warm mist. To Nancy they were two great clues. . . .

"Bess? George?" Nancy called. "I just found a bunch of tissues and a vaporizer."

"So?" George asked.

Nancy looked at her friends and smiled. "So Henderson doesn't have a stomachache," she declared. "He has a cold!"

Chapter

7

COLD CASE

"So are you saying Henderson didn't eat the chocolate turkey, Nancy?" Bess asked.

Nancy was about to answer when—

"Turkey, turkey, gobble-gobble, eat 'em up!" a voice squawked. "Raaaak!"

Nancy, Bess, and George shrieked as a parrot soared into the room over their heads. The big parrot, whose feathers were blue and green, squawked before swooping down over the fruit platter!

Nancy watched as the parrot pecked at the fruit. "So that's where the blue and green feathers in Henderson's room came from," she said with a smile. "He has a parrot!"

"A green-winged macaw to be exact," Henderson's voice said.

The girls turned toward the door. A red-nosed Henderson walked into his room wearing sweats and dinosaur-head slippers.

"My mom said you brought me fruit," Henderson said with a sniff. "Thanks. I could use the vitamin C."

"You're welcome," George said, nodding at the pecking parrot. "I hope you don't mind sharing with beaky breath over there."

"His name is Rocky," Henderson said, "after my dad's most popular ice cream flavor— Chocolate Rocky Road."

Nancy decided to tell Henderson the reason they had come. "Speaking of chocolate," she said, "we were looking around your room for a choco-late turkey."

"Chocolate turkey?" Henderson asked. "What chocolate turkey?"

"The chocolate turkey that went missing from Classy Coco," Bess replied, "before the Turkey Trot yesterday."

Henderson scrunched his brow trying to understand. "So you thought I took it?" he asked. "Why would you think that?"

"You were mad at Anna Epicure, Henderson," Nancy explained, "for saying not-so-nice things about your dad's hot chocolate."

"I was mad," Henderson admitted, "but I would never take something that wasn't mine."

Nancy, Bess, and George traded looks. They pretty much believed Henderson. There was just one question left to be asked. . . .

"Where were you yesterday morning before the Turkey Trot?" Nancy asked.

"Where do you think I was?" Henderson asked with a sniff. "In bed sneezing and honking my nose off, that's where!"

Nancy heard the hiss of the vaporizer. "I believe him," she told her friends.

"Me too," Bess whispered.

But George shook her head. "Not so fast," she said. "Henderson could have caught the cold yesterday afternoon. He could have felt fine in the morning when the turkey went missing."

"Come to think of it," Bess said, "maybe Henderson took Rocky with him to Classy Coco. Why else would those blue and green feathers be on the floor?"

"What would Rocky be doing there?" Nancy asked.

"Maybe the parrot was Henderson's lookout!" George said.

"Stop that!" Henderson said. "I repeat—I am not your chocolate turkey thief!"

Henderson blew his nose, then added, "All I did

yesterday morning was watch the Thanksgiving Parade on TV."

The Thanksgiving Parade!

Nancy's eyes lit up. The parade could be Henderson's excuse for being home!

"If you watched the parade, then you saw the Ginger Girls," Nancy said. "What kind of float did they sing on?"

"A pirate ship," Henderson replied. "I'm not a Ginger Girls fan, but that was pretty cool."

"What song did they sing?" Bess quizzed.

"I don't remember," Henderson said. "I watched the parade to see the Danger Dog balloon, not the Ginger Girls!"

Rocky picked his feathery head up from the fruit platter. He circled his neck and began to sing: "All aboooooard the ship of loooooove! Arrrrk! All aboooooard!"

"Rocky's singing 'Ship of Love!'" Bess said excitedly. "That's the song the Ginger Girls sang in the parade!"

"Rocky was watching the parade too," Nancy

said. "He couldn't have been at Classy Coco yesterday morning either."

"Any other questions, Clue Crew?" Henderson asked.

"Just one," Nancy said. "What did you mean when you said you'd show Anna?"

Henderson smiled. "Follow me," he said.

Nancy, Bess, and George followed Henderson to the window in his room. Outside was his dad's truck and a line of kids waiting to buy hot chocolate and cookies.

"I just wanted to show Anna that my dad's Minty Martian hot chocolate would be a hit," Henderson explained. "And as you can see, it is!"

Rocky ruffled his feathers. "Minty Martian, Minty Martian!" he squawked. "Out of this world! Arrrrrk!"

Nancy giggled as the parrot rolled his feathery head in a circle. "Thanks for being a good sport, Henderson," she said.

"No problem," Henderson said. He threw back his head and, "Ah . . . ah . . . ah . . . ahhhh—"

The girls watched Henderson sneeze into his hand. Then he lifted it to high-five. Gross!

"Um . . . we'd better go," George blurted.

"Feel better!" Bess called as they headed for the door.

The Clue Crew said goodbye to Mrs. Murphy before leaving the house. Nancy was happy to cross Henderson's name off of her suspect list.

"Who's left?" Bess asked.

Nancy pointed to the last name on their suspect list.

"The Choco Chewers Club," she replied. "They would do anything for chocolate."

"Plus they wore blue and green feathers around their necks to the Turkey Trot!" George pointed out.

"Tomorrow is Saturday, when the Choco Chewers have their club meeting," Nancy said as she closed her clue book. "Let's go to their clubhouse and see what we can find out."

"How do we find their clubhouse?" Bess said.

"I heard Hazel bragging at school that she has

her own Choco Chewers Club blog," George said. "Maybe she wrote about their clubhouse."

"I can look up Hazel's blog tonight," Nancy said. "If the clubhouse is nearby, we'll walk there together tomorrow."

"Should we bring them fruit too?" George joked.

"Only if it's dipped in chocolate." Bess giggled.

"Nancy, we're leaving in ten minutes!" Mr. Drew called from downstairs. "We don't want to be late for the movie."

"Okay, Daddy!" Nancy called back. "I just need to look something up real fast."

Nancy was up in her room at her computer. Chocolate Chip sat at her side, wagging her tail.

"Here's Hazel's blog, Chip," Nancy said, pointing to the screen. "She wrote that her clubhouse is in her own backyard!"

Nancy was about to close the site when she noticed something on Hazel's blog. It was a group picture of the Choco Chewers Club—next to a giant chocolate turkey. Scrolling down, Nancy read what was written underneath:

"We didn't have to WIN the chocolate turkey at Classy Coco because look what we have. BOOM!"

Nancy leaned forward to stare at the chocolate turkey in the picture. "Chip, it's true, it's true!" she told her dog. "The Choco Chewers aren't just chocoholics—they could be choco bandits!"

Chapter

8

SWEET TOOTH SLEUTHS

"Great find, Nancy," Bess said. "But how do we know the chocolate turkey in this picture is the chocolate turkey from Classy Coco?"

It was Saturday morning. The Clue Crew sat at Nancy's computer checking out Hazel's Choco Chewers blog and picture.

"We don't know," Nancy said. "That's why we have to see it with our own eyes."

"Then I hope we have X-ray vision," George

joked, "because the chocolate turkey is probably in the club's stomachs by now."

"Maybe not," Nancy said, scrolling down to something else Hazel wrote. "It says here that the club is cutting the chocolate turkey today at one o'clock."

"It's twelve thirty now," Bess said, glancing at her watch. "If the club didn't cut the chocolate turkey yet, they didn't eat it yet!"

"We have a half hour to get to the clubhouse," George said. "But what if Hazel and the others don't let us inside?"

"It's not like we belong to the Choco Chewers Club," Bess said.

Nancy smiled at her puppy, Chip, playing with one of her slippers. "I think I just thought of a way," she said slowly.

The girls rushed to Hazel's house. On the way they walked up Main Street, busy with Saturday shoppers. They saw Anna Epicure standing in front of Classy Coco. She held a tray filled with paper cups, smiling as kids lined up to take one.

"What's in the cups?" George asked a boy as he walked by.

"Yummy hot cocoa," the boy said, lifting his cup. "The lady who owns the store is giving out free samples."

"Free samples?" Nancy said after the boy walked away. "Anna said she never gives out free samples."

"She said she never makes hot chocolate, either," George pointed out.

"She does now!" Bess said with a smile. "What are we waiting for? Let's get some."

"No," Nancy said, shaking her head. "We have to get to the Choco Chewers clubhouse before they eat the chocolate turkey."

Nancy, Bess, and George walked the short distance to the Hookstratten house. Hazel's dad directed them to the backyard.

When the girls saw the Choco Chewer's clubhouse their jaws dropped. It was the size of a large tool shed but looked nothing like one. It was decorated to look like it was built out of chocolate bars!

"Sweet!" George exclaimed.

"Not really," Bess said with a frown. "A candy house didn't work out so great for Hansel and Gretel."

Nancy led the way to the clubhouse. Using the chocolate-pretzel-shaped door knocker, she rapped on the door. After a few seconds, Hazel opened the door. Other club members stood behind her, looking over her shoulders.

"Hi, guys," Nancy said with a smile. "We read about the chocolate turkey you're about to eat."

"Mind if we take a look?" George asked.

Lester squeezed next to Hazel at the door. "A look?" he said. "One look at our chocolate turkey and you're going to want to eat it!"

"Only club members can taste our chocolate turkey," Hazel said.

"Then may we join your club?" Nancy asked.

"It depends," Hazel said. "How much do you like chocolate?"

Nancy was expecting that question. "I like chocolate so much," she said, "that I named my puppy Chocolate Chip!"

"So what?" Lester said. "My dog's name is Prince. That doesn't make me a king."

Hazel and the others murmured in agreement.

"Give me a break!" George cried. "We don't have to taste your chocolate turkey."

"But, George," Bess whispered. "We have to—"

"Anna Epicure is giving out free samples of hot chocolate at Classy Coco," George told the club. "It's probably way better than your chocolate turkey."

Nancy suddenly knew what George had in

mind. "The hot chocolate is free today," she told the club. "I'll bet it's sweet, thick, and real chocolaty!"

"Thick . . . sweet . . . chocolaty?" Hazel repeated. She turned to the other club members who were also swooning. "The chocolate turkey will have to wait. Next stop: Classy Coco!"

Nancy, Bess, and George stepped away from the door to let the Choco Chewers dash out. After the club members rounded the house, the girls slipped inside the clubhouse.

"Good thinking, George," Nancy said with a smile. "Now, where is that chocolate turkey?"

The clubhouse had several beanbag chairs shaped like chocolate candies and posters on the walls with sayings like, "Stay Calm and Eat Chocolate" and "Follow That Bunny—He Has Chocolate!"

Stacked on a shelf were hard metal molds of all shapes and sizes. Nancy held up one shaped like a horse and said, "I'll bet the Choco Chewers use these to make their own chocolate."

George opened a small freezer. Inside were molded chocolates and chocolate lollipops. "Here are some," she said. "That dark-chocolate sneaker looks pretty good—"

"Nancy, George, I found it," Bess interrupted. "I found the chocolate turkey from the picture!"

Nancy and George hurried over to Bess. She was standing next to a chocolate turkey set up on a stool in the corner.

"How do we know if that's the missing turkey?" Nancy asked.

"We got to taste the Classy Coco turkey before it went missing," George said. "If we taste this turkey, we'll know if it's a match."

"But how?" Bess asked. "It's not like we can break off a piece."

George's eyes darted around the clubhouse. "Maybe we don't have to," she said.

Nancy watched as George headed toward a stainless-steel pot. The pot stood on the floor. It was the biggest Nancy had ever seen. It was half the size of Nancy!

Looking into it, George said, "This is half-filled with melted chocolate. Maybe the Choco Chewers melted the turkey from Anna's store to make their own over there!"

"Why would they do all that just to make another chocolate turkey?" Nancy wondered.

George leaned over the rim of the pot to dip her finger into the cooled chocolate. After giving it a lick, she said, "This chocolate is good, but not as good as the missing turkey."

Bess didn't like to get messy, but she couldn't resist a taste. She reached her finger down toward the melted chocolate but gasped as her bracelet fell into the pot!

"I have to get my bracelet out!" Bess cried. "It has little autumn leaf beads. It's my favorite!"

"Don't reach for it, Bess," Nancy warned. "You might fall in too."

"I have longer arms," George said. "I'll do it."

Nancy and Bess stood back as George leaned over the rim of the pot. She stretched her arm down for the bracelet but grunted when she couldn't reach it.

"Keep trying, George," Bess cried. "I have matching earrings—"

"Okay, okay," George said. She reached in further, further, further until—SPLAT!

Nancy and Bess shrieked. George had fallen headfirst into the pot of melted chocolate!

Chapter

9

CHOCO-LOT!

"Um . . . did you find my bracelet, George?" Bess asked.

George rose from the pot, her face and hair dripping with chocolate. "Here," she muttered, tossing the chocolate-covered bracelet to Bess.

Nancy watched George try to climb out of the pot, but she kept slipping back down. "Do you need help, George?" she asked.

"Why don't we lend a hand?" a voice asked.

Nancy froze. She knew the voice belonged to

Hazel. The girls looked toward the door to see her and the other Choco Chewers filing into the clubhouse.

"We thought you were with us when we went for hot chocolate!" Hazel said angrily. She pointed to George in the pot. "Instead you're eating our chocolate!"

"Does it look like I'm eating?" George demanded.

"Hazel, we didn't come to eat chocolate," Nancy explained. "We were looking for the missing chocolate turkey from Classy Coco."

"We thought your chocolate turkey might be it," Bess said. "But we figured out that it isn't."

"The hard way," George sighed. "Can somebody please help me out?"

With the help of the Choco Chewers, George climbed out of the pot. Nancy and Bess used wads of paper towels to help clean up the mess.

"Do you really make your own chocolate?" Nancy asked as she scrubbed a spot on the floor.

"You bet," Hazel said. "My dad melts chocolate

in our garage. After it cools down a bit, we pour it into molds, freeze them, and—"

"Eat them!" Lester said. "That's the best part!"

George noticed a chocolate mustache on Lester. "How was Anna's hot chocolate?" she asked.

"Awesome!" Lester declared, licking his upper lip. "It tasted exactly like a melted chocolate bar."

Gillian held out a paper cup. "Would you like to taste it?" she asked the Clue Crew. "It's so rich I couldn't finish it."

"I'll try it, thanks!" Bess said, reaching for the cup.

Before Bess could take a sip, Hazel said, "I've decided naming a dog Chocolate Chip is a pretty big deal. Do you guys want to taste our chocolate turkey?"

"We're about to cut it," Lester said excitedly. "With Mr. Hookstratten's help, of course."

"Thanks, but no thanks," George said, chocolate dripping down her forehead. "I've had enough chocolate for the day. Sorry I ruined this batch, you guys."

"It's okay," Gillian said. "We have tons more where that came from."

The Clue Crew thanked the Choco Chewers and left the clubhouse. Once outside, Bess took a sip of the hot chocolate. Nancy could see her eyes light up.

"Does Anna's hot chocolate really taste like a melted chocolate bar?" Nancy asked.

"Better!" Bess declared. "It tastes like the chocolate turkey from Classy Coco."

"You mean the pieces that broke off?" George asked. "The ones we tasted?"

"Taste it for yourself," Bess said, holding out the cup.

George wasn't planning on more chocolate, but she took a sip anyway.

"Whoa!" George exclaimed. "That tastes just like the chocolate turkey from Classy Coco."

As Nancy took a sip she had a thought.

"What's up, Nancy? You have that look on your face," Bess told her.

"So, Clue Crew, I think I have the answer," Nancy said. She swallowed the last delicious drop of hot chocolate and continued. "Next stop: Classy Coco!"

George shook her head, her chocolate-crusted curls bouncing. "Nuh-uh, Nancy," she said. "Next stop for me is a shower!"

Nancy, Bess, and George headed to the Fayne house. After George was done showering, she threw her clothes into the laundry hamper.

"Your hair is still wet, George," Bess pointed out. "Don't you blow-dry and style it?"

"I prefer to drip-dry, thanks," George said. "Now let's go to Classy Coco and look for some clues."

"If Anna lets us inside," Nancy said hopefully.

The Clue Crew practically ran all the way to Main Street. Luckily, Anna was still giving out samples in front of her store.

The girls pretended to join the line of kids

waiting for samples. When no one was looking, they slipped through the open door into the store.

"That's weird," Nancy said as they looked around. "There are no chocolates anywhere in the store."

George pointed to the floor. "No more blue and green feathers either."

"Anna probably swept them up already," Bess said. "But where did all the chocolate go?"

Nancy pointed to a closed door behind the counter. "It could be in the back room," she said. "Let's check it out."

George opened the door. As the girls filed into the back, they all gasped. Stretched out before them on a large table was a sea of paper cups filled with hot chocolate!

"Holy ravioli!" George exclaimed.

"Look at all that melted chocolate!" Bess gasped.

Nancy walked along the table, gazing at about a hundred filled cups.

Clue Crew—and
YOU!

Ready to think like Nancy, Bess, and George and help solve the case of the missing chocolate turkey? Or turn the page to find out what happened!

1. The Clue Crew ruled out Henderson, Shelby, and the Choco Chewers Club as suspects. Can you think of anyone they may have left out? Write one or more on a piece of paper.

2. Nancy sees almost a hundred cups of hot chocolate in Classy Coco. Where do you think all that melted chocolate came from? Write your answer on a piece of paper.

3. Many times detectives use their eyes and ears to solve cases. How are Nancy, Bess, and George using their taste buds? Write your thoughts on a piece of a paper.

Chapter

10

TALKING TURKEY

Nancy swept her hand over the cups and said, "All this melted chocolate came from all the chocolate in Anna's store! The chocolate turkey wasn't stolen. It was melted! Just like all her other chocolate!"

"Children are not allowed back here," a voice declared.

Nancy, Bess, and George looked up to see Anna Epicure, an empty tray in her hand.

"I need more hot chocolate," Anna said. "So

if you girls will please leave—"

"We thought you didn't make hot chocolate," George cut in.

"Or give out samples," Bess added.

Anna walked over to the table. "This isn't just hot chocolate, girls. These are the finest hot chocolates from all over the world."

"You mean from all over your store," Nancy stated. "Which cups are from the melted chocolate turkey, Anna?"

"M-melted?" Anna stammered. "Why on earth would I melt my own chocolate?"

"To make hot chocolate," Bess said cheerily. "It's okay if you were jealous of Mr. Drippy."

Anna stared at Nancy, Bess, and George. "Jealous?" she scoffed. "Of green hot chocolate and marshmallows?"

"Then tell us the real reason, please," Nancy said.

"Yeah, Anna," George said. "Time to talk turkey."

Anna heaved a big sigh as she placed her tray

down. "Oh, all right," she said. "My chocolates did melt, but not the way you think."

"What do you mean?" Nancy asked.

"Each day before I leave the store I turn on the air conditioner," Anna explained, "so the chocolates will stay cool and not get soft."

She pointed to the thermostat on the wall. "But on Wednesday night, the night before Thanksgiving, I turned on the heat. All the way up!"

"Oh no!" Bess gasped.

Nancy remembered what happened to the Choco Chewers costumes in the sun. "So the chocolate melted?" she asked.

"Inside their plastic bags," Anna said. "It was like walking into a store filled with chocolate water balloons!"

Nancy's eyes widened at the thought. "If it was an accident," she asked, "why didn't you tell Mayor Strong?"

"I didn't want to admit my mistake," Anna

said. "So I poured the melted chocolate into dainty little cups and—"

"And had kids drink the evidence," George cut in.

"I suppose," Anna sighed. "I so wanted to present my chocolate turkey at the Turkey Trot. I even bought a feather boa just for the occasion."

"Feather boa?" Nancy asked.

"Oh, yes!" Anna exclaimed. Reaching under the table she pulled out a feathered scarf and wrapped it around her neck. "What do you think, girls?"

A few feathers fluttered off onto the floor. Blue and green feathers!

"I think that explains the feathers on the floor," Nancy said with a smile.

But Anna wasn't smiling as she said, "I feel bad for blaming you kids for the melted turkey, and for making fun of Mr. Drippy's hot chocolate."

"You do?" Bess asked.

Anna nodded and said, "I finally see how

everyone loves hot chocolate, especially you children."

"So will kids be allowed in your store again?" Nancy asked excitedly.

"Of course," Anna said before heaving another sigh. "But I'm afraid no one will want to come to Classy Coco after knowing what I did."

At that moment a familiar tune jingled outside. It was the sound of the Mr. Drippy truck—and it gave Nancy an idea.

"Maybe people don't have to come back to your store, Anna," Nancy said with a smile. "At least not right away."

"What do you mean?" Anna asked.

"Yeah, Nancy," George said. "What do you mean?"

Nancy's smile grew wider as she said, "You'll see!"

"Come and get it, kids!" Mr. Murphy shouted from his truck. "We've got a new fall flavor called Candy Cornucopia!"

Henderson stood next to his dad. "It's orange hot chocolate with yellow marshmallows," he added, "and it tastes as good as it looks!"

Nancy, Bess, and George gathered at the window of the Mr. Drippy truck. It had been a week since the Clue Crew solved the case of the melted chocolate turkey.

"We'll each have a cup, please," Nancy said, "plus one chocolate brownie to share."

"Excellent choice," Henderson said. He turned toward the back of the truck and called out, "Anna—you're on!"

Anna stepped up behind the window, her feathered boa wrapped around her neck. Holding a paper bag, she said, "One chocolate brownie imported from my kitchen. Bon-bon appétit!"

"Thank you, Anna!" Nancy said.

Holding their treats, Nancy, Bess, and George walked away from the Mr. Drippy truck.

"Anna looks so happy," Bess said. "Teaming

up with Mr. Drippy until her store is back in business was a great idea."

"How did you figure that out, Nancy?" George asked.

"Because there's nothing like teamwork," Nancy said with a big smile. "And if anyone knows about teamwork—it's the Clue Crew!"

Test your detective skills with
even more Clue Book mysteries:

**Nancy Drew Clue Book #13:
Puppy Love Prank**

"Stop!" Bess Marvin shouted as she came to a halt. "We forgot something superimportant!"

Nancy Drew stopped walking too. So did her other best friend, George Fayne. All three girls were carrying plastic bins filled with treats for the wedding they were going to today.

"We didn't forget to dress up for the wedding," Nancy told Bess. "We're both wearing party dresses and George is wearing a tuxedo T-shirt."

"Yes, but every wedding has something old, something new, something borrowed, and something blue," Bess explained. "We don't have any of those."

George raised a foot and said, "My sneakers are old."

Bess rolled her eyes at George's grubby, frayed sneaker. "That's for sure," she sighed.

"And I'm wearing Hannah's sparkly poodle pin," Nancy said. "That's borrowed."

"Your dress is new, Bess," George said, "like everything else you wear."

"Very funny," Bess said with a smirk.

Nancy giggled. She had known Bess and George forever but still couldn't believe they were cousins.

Bess washed her long blond hair almost every morning, painted her nails pink, and had a closet filled with stylin' clothes. The only time George trimmed her nails was when they grew too long for her computer keyboard or softball catcher's mitt.

But like Nancy, Bess and George were great at solving mysteries. That's why all three friends had their own detective club called the Clue Crew. Nancy even had a special notebook where she wrote down all their suspects and clues!

"We need something blue, you guys," Bess insisted. "It's a wedding tradition."

George's dark curls bounced as she shook her head. "It's a dog wedding, Bess," she pointed out. "There's nothing traditional about that."

Nancy, Bess, and George stood outside Mayor Strong's mansion, where the dog wedding would take place. Getting married were Helga and Horatio, the fluffy white bichon frises of Mrs. Ainsworth, the richest woman in River Heights.

"Let's not forget the main reason for this wedding," Nancy said. "To let everyone know about the pet shelter Waggamuffins and all the dogs who need homes."

"And because my mom is catering the wedding," George said proudly. "We get to walk three of those dogs down the aisles as brides-mutts. How cool is that?"

"It would be even cooler," Bess sighed, "if we could find something blue."

Nancy, Bess, and George carried the bins filled with doggy cupcakes up the path to the mayor's mansion. Mrs. Fayne and her staff unloaded the catering truck to one side of the driveway.

When Mrs. Fayne saw the girls, she smiled. "Thanks for bringing the pupcakes, girls," she said. "You can put the bins on the rolling cart."

"Good," George said with a grin. "These cupcakes may be for dogs, but there're enough to feed ten elephants!"

"Where are Helga and Horatio, Mrs. Fayne?" Nancy asked while stacking the bins. "We'd love to meet them before the wedding!"

"Mayor Strong arranged a special room for the dogs," Mrs. Fayne said, pointing to a door at the back of the house. "It even has its own entrance."

Mrs. Fayne returned to her work and the girls turned toward the door. Nancy brushed aside her reddish-blond bangs to read a sign on the door. It read: PRIVATE.

"Now we can't go inside the room to meet Helga and Horatio," Nancy said, disappointed.

"Who says we can't?" George asked. She walked to the rolling cart, grabbed two pupcakes, and said, "Special delivery for Helga and Horatio!"

Nancy knocked three times on the door. They waited until a woman's voice called, "Enter!"

Bess opened the door. As they stepped inside, the girls looked around the room. The first thing they noticed was a doggy-size wedding dress and tuxedo hanging on a rack. Standing by the rack and waving a steamer was a boy of about nine or ten.

A silver-haired woman sat on a velvet throne-like chair holding two fluffy white dogs. "You missed a wrinkle on the left suspender, Ludlow," she told the boy. "Keep steaming, please."

"Yes, Grandma," Ludlow replied.

Nancy guessed the woman was Mrs. Ainsworth. The dogs had to be Helga and Horatio!

"Hello, Mrs. Ainsworth," Nancy said. "We've

come with pupcakes for the happy couple. They're cupcakes baked for dogs—"

"Not these dogs," Mrs. Ainsworth cut in. "What would my babies do if they got cream on their clean fur?"

"They'd lick it off," George said with a shrug. "They're dogs, right?"

Mrs. Ainsworth didn't laugh, but Ludlow did. He blushed when he noticed Nancy, Bess, and George looking his way.

"Do you go to River Heights Elementary School?" Nancy asked nicely. "You don't look familiar."

"That's because I live in the next town," Ludlow said, turning off the steamer. "I'm helping my grandmother with the wedding."

"And making sure my babies stay perfectly groomed on their big day," Mrs. Ainsworth added.

"Did someone say 'groomed'?" a voice piped in.

Nancy, Bess, and George turned to see a couple at the door. Each wore crisp black smocks over tailored black pants. They carried silver tote bags over their shoulders.

"And you are?" Mrs. Ainsworth asked.

"I'm Kelly Davis and this is my husband Kevin," the woman said, "Better known as the Va-Va-Groom glam squad!"

"I know what a glam squad is," Bess said excitedly. "You make people beautiful, right?"

"We make dogs beautiful," Kevin stated.

"Va-Va-Groom is the fancy new dog salon on Main Street," Kelly added.

"I heard about Va-Va-Groom," Nancy said. "It's way too fancy for my dog, Chip."

In a flash Kelly handed Nancy a piece of paper and said, "Take this coupon. It's for twenty dollars off a soothing sports pawdicure including tax and tip."

"Pawdicure?" Nancy asked.

"Now," Kelly said, smiling at Helga and Horatio. "Where do we begin?"

"By leaving, please," Mrs. Ainsworth said. "I never called for groomers."

"That's because I did!" Mayor Strong boomed as he burst into the room following a huge hairy dog. "For my dog, Huey."

Nancy wanted to squeeze her nose but didn't. Huey smelled a bit ewie. Meanwhile the glam squad stared at the mayor's dog.

"Would your dog like a soothing massage, Mayor Strong?" Kevin asked. "Or colorful stencils on his rather matted fur?"

"Nah," Mayor Strong said. "Huey rolled in something stinky. Dig out the dead leaves or whatever else you find in there."

The mayor gave his dog a final pat. "Oh, and clean the gunk out of his ears, too. So he can hear me whistle."

Nancy could tell the glam squad was horrified by the mayor's request. In a panic the couple turned to Mrs. Ainsworth.

"Surely there's something we can do for the bride and groom!" Kelly said. "Instead of Huey?"

"Pleeeeease?" Kevin squeaked.

"I'm afraid not," Mrs. Ainsworth said. "Helga

and Horatio were groomed this morning by Mr. Clippy of Canine Couture."

"You mean the celebrity dog groomer to the stars?" Kelly gasped. "His salon is in Chicago!"

"Mr. Clippy makes house calls," Mrs. Ainsworth says, "in his private helicopter."

Nancy could hear Kelly and Kevin growl under their breaths. Just like the dogs they groomed.

"I'll leave Huey in your good hands," Mayor Strong said, sticking the leash between Kelly's clenched fist. "See you all at the wedding!"

Kelly and Kevin stood frozen as the mayor left the room. George turned to the couple. "Take these for Huey," she said, holding out the two pupcakes. "I'm sure he won't mind frosting on his fur."

"It would be an improvement," Kevin muttered.

"Woof!" Huey barked.

Kelly steered Huey toward the door. On their way out Nancy heard her say, "Kevin, I think we've just been dogged!"

Nancy didn't know what Kelly meant by that. But she did know one thing: The Va-Va-Groom glam squad was mad!

"Should I shut the door, Grandma?" Ludlow asked.

"Don't bother, dear," Mrs. Ainsworth said. "It's eleven o'clock and time for you to walk Helga and Horatio."

Nancy, Bess, and George listened to Mrs. Ainsworth give Ludlow special walking instructions: Walk Helga and Horatio for a half an hour away from the guests. Then bring the dogs back to their room for an hour's rest before the wedding at twelve thirty.

While Ludlow fetched the dogs' leashes Nancy had an idea. . . .

"Why don't you walk Helga and Horatio in the park across the street, Ludlow?" Nancy asked. "My dog, Chip, loves it there!"

"The park?" Mrs. Ainsworth demanded. "Do my babies look like they chase squirrels?"

Suddenly—MEOW! Nancy, Bess, and

George whirled around. Standing in the doorway was a cat wearing a ruffled collar and lacy bonnet. Helga and Horatio growled at the little cat, then leaped off of Mrs. Ainsworth's lap. Yapping all the way, the dogs chased the cat out the door!

"They may not chase squirrels," George exclaimed, pointing outside. "But look at them go after that cat!"

Mrs. Ainsworth jumped up from her chair, wringing her hands. "I told Mayor Strong not to invite cats to this wedding! Somebody bring back my babies!"

BRIDE AND GLOOM

"On it, Mrs. Ainsworth!" Nancy said.

With Ludlow running behind them, Nancy, Bess, and George chased the dogs that chased the cat. They charged through the mayor's garden, beneath a lawn sprinkler and through Mrs. Fayne's catering tent.

"Whoa!" George shouted as the three animals scampered under the table holding the wedding cake. The tall cake decorated with a dog-couple topper trembled this way and that, but luckily didn't fall.

Helga and Horatio chased the cat out of the tent. Ludlow caught up with the dogs, snapping on their leashes and shouting, "Gotcha!"

Ludlow hurried off with both dogs. Meowing, the cat jumped into the open arms of a girl dressed in a fancy dress and straw hat. "There you are, Snowball," she cooed. "I was wondering where you went!"

Nancy, Bess, and George recognized the girl and her two friends, who walked over carrying cats too.

The three were in the fourth grade and best friends because of their love of cats. They even gave themselves cat nicknames to prove it: Kitty McNulty, Ally Katz, and Purr-cilla Chang. Everyone at school called them the Kitty Klub!

"Your cats look so pretty in their frilly collars and bonnets!" Bess said with a smile.

The Kitty Klub refused to smile back.

"Mayor Strong just told us that cats aren't allowed at the wedding," Kitty said.

"We want to know why," Ally demanded.

"I know why," George replied. "Cats plus dogs equal zoomies. You just saw for yourself."

"But we got something from the registry list!" Purr-cilla complained, holding a chew toy with her free hand. She gave it a squeak and said, "See?"

"Sorry," Nancy said gently. "But Mrs. Ainsworth, Helga and Horatio's owner, said the same."

The Kitty Klub traded frowns.

"Who ever heard of a dog wedding, anyway?" Kitty grumbled as they turned to leave.

"Yeah, well, somebody is about to hear from us," Purr-cilla said, "because I just got an idea!"

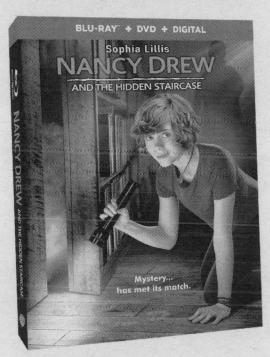